1 Stranger

BE CAUTIOUS AROUND STRANGERS.

2 Traffic

TRAFFIC RULES AND STAYING SAFE.

3 Boundaries

IMPORTANCE OF PERSONAL BOUNDARIES AND HOW TO SET THEM.

4 Fire

KNOW HOW TO STAY SAFE IN CASE OF A FIRE EMERGENCY.

5 Water

HOW TO STAY SAFE WHILE SWIMMING.

6 Internet

HOW TO STAY SAFE WHILE USING THE INTERNET.

7 First Aid

HOW TO RESPOND IN CASE OF AN EMERGENCY.

8 Playground

HOW TO STAY SAFE WHILE PLAYING.

9 Home

HOW TO STAY SAFE WHILE AT HOME.

10 Emergency

KNOWG WHAT TO DO IN CASE OF AN EMERGENCY.

STRANGER AWARENESS

The importance of being cautious when approached by strangers, even if they seem friendly.

The Tricky Stranger

A boy named Max loved to ride his bike around the neighborhood. One day, as he was riding down the street, a man pulled over in his car and rolled down the window.

"Hey there, little guy!" The man said it with a friendly smile. "I'm new to the area, and I'm a bit lost. Can you help me find my way?"

Max felt a bit nervous but did not want to be rude. He approached the car cautiously, and the man showed him a map. But as Max leaned forward to look, he noticed something strange. The man's other hand was in his pocket, and Max could not see what he was doing.

Suddenly, Max remembered his parents' advice about stranger danger. He thanked the man and quickly rode away on his bike. As he looked back, he saw the man's car speed off in the opposite direction.

Max realized that he had been approached by a tricky stranger who might have had bad intentions. He felt proud of himself for being cautious and remembering to never go with strangers, even if they seemed friendly.

From that day on, Max was always careful around strangers and never let his guard down. He knew that his safety was his top priority, and he would do anything to protect himself from danger.

TRAFFIC SAFETY

The importance of following traffic rules and staying safe while crossing the street.

The Traffic Light Hero

A boy named Alex loved to ride his scooter to the park. On his way there, he always had to cross a busy street. But Alex knew that he needed to be careful when crossing the street and always looked both ways before crossing.

One day, as Alex was about to cross the street, he noticed that the traffic light had turned red. He stopped in his tracks and waited patiently for the light to turn green.

As he waited, he noticed a little girl who was about to cross the street without looking. Alex quickly sprang into action and yelled, "Stop! Do not cross the street yet!"

The little girl stopped and looked at Alex in surprise. Alex quickly explained to her that she needed to wait until the traffic light turned green and look both ways before crossing. He showed her how to do it, and they safely crossed the street together.

As they made it safely to the other side, Alex felt proud of himself for being a traffic light hero. He knew that following traffic rules and staying safe while crossing the street were especially important.

From that day on, Alex always made sure to follow the traffic rules and help others do the same. He knew that being a hero was all about helping others and making the world a safer place.

PERSONAL BOUNDARIES

The importance of safe touch and personal boundaries and how to set them.

My Body, My Rules

There was a girl named Lily who loved playing with her friends. One day, a new friend named Jack came to play with them. Jack was a bit rough and always wanted to play rough games that made Lily feel uncomfortable.

One day, Jack tried to play a game that involved touching Lily in a way that she did not like. Lily felt uncomfortable and knew that she needed to set a boundary.

She told Jack, "Stop! I don't like to be touched that way." Jack was a bit surprised and asked why. Lily explained that it made her feel uncomfortable and that she did not want to play that game.

Jack apologized and said he did not know. He suggested they play a different game that did not involve touching each other. Lily felt much better and was proud of herself for setting a personal boundary.

From that day on, Lily knew that it was important to set personal boundaries and to speak up when someone was making her feel uncomfortable. She also learned that it was okay to say no and that she did not have to do anything she did not want to do.

FIRE SAFETY

The importance of having a fire safety plan
and knowing how to stay safe in case of a fire
emergency.

The Fire Safety Plan

There was a family who lived in a house in the suburbs. One day, the youngest member of the family, a boy named Max, asked his parents what would happen if a fire broke out in their house.

His parents explained to him that they had a fire safety plan in place and showed him the smoke alarms and fire extinguishers in the house. They also explained to him that in the event of a fire, they would all need to stay calm and follow the plan.

A few days later, while Max was sleeping, he was woken up by a loud beeping sound. He realized that the smoke alarm was going off and quickly woke up his family.

Everyone quickly followed the fire safety plan. They crawled under the smoke and made their way to the designated meeting spot outside. Max's parents called the fire department while Max made sure everyone was accounted for. The fire department arrived quickly and put out the fire. Thanks to their fire safety plan, everyone was safe, and the damage to their house was minimal.

Max learned that it was important to always have a fire safety plan and to know what to do in case of a fire emergency. He also realized that practicing fire safety was important not just for his own safety but for the safety of his family and home.

From that day on, Max made sure to always check the smoke alarms and fire extinguishers in their house and to review their fire safety plan regularly. He knew that being prepared was the best way to stay safe in case of a fire emergency.

WATER SAFETY

The importance of water safety and how to stay safe while swimming.

The Water Adventure

A girl named Sara loved to swim. She was excited to go on a trip to the beach with her family and could not wait to jump into the water.

As soon as they arrived at the beach, Sara ran into the water. She was having so much fun splashing around that she did not notice the waves getting bigger.

Suddenly, she felt herself getting pulled away from the shore. She started to panic and did not know what to do.

Luckily, Sara had learned about water safety at school and knew what to do in case of an emergency. She stayed calm and started to swim parallel to the shore, not against the waves. This helped her escape from the strong currents.

Sara swam back to the shore, where her parents were waiting for her. They were so proud of her for staying calm and knowing what to do in case of an emergency.

From that day on, Sara knew that it was important to always practice water safety and never underestimate the power of the ocean. She made sure to always swim in designated areas and to never swim alone.

INTERNET SAFETY

The importance of internet safety and how to stay safe while using the internet.

The Internet Safety Adventure

There was a boy named Max who loved to play games and watch videos online. One day, he received a message from someone he did not know who wanted to be his friend.

Max was excited and accepted the friend request. However, he soon realized that the person was not who they said they were. They started to ask him personal questions and wanted to meet up with him in person.

Max felt scared and knew that he needed to tell his parents. His parents taught him about internet safety and how to stay safe while using the internet. They told him to never share personal information with someone he did not know and to always tell an adult if he felt uncomfortable.

Thanks to his parents' guidance, Max knew what to do. He stopped talking to the stranger and told his parents what had happened.

From that day on, Max made sure to always practice internet safety. He learned about other ways to stay safe, such as using a strong password, not clicking on suspicious links, and not downloading anything without his parents' permission.

Max felt empowered knowing that he could have fun on the internet while also staying safe. He knew that internet safety was important for everyone and that he could help his friends stay safe too.

FIRST AID

The importance of knowing basic first aid and how to respond in case of an emergency.

The First Aid Adventure

A boy named Ben loved to explore the outdoors. One day, he was hiking in the woods with his family when he suddenly tripped and fell.

He scraped his knee, and it started to bleed a lot. Ben's mom quickly assessed the wound and applied pressure to stop the bleeding. She then cleaned the wound and put a bandage on it.

Ben was scared and in pain, but his mom's quick thinking and knowledge of basic first aid helped him feel better.

From that day on, Ben knew that it was important to know basic first aid and how to respond in case of an emergency. He learned about diverse types of wounds and how to clean and bandage them. He also learned about CPR and how to perform it in case of a cardiac emergency.

Thanks to his mom's quick response and knowledge of first aid, Ben was able to quickly recover and get back to his outdoor adventures. He felt proud of himself for knowing what to do in case of an emergency and was grateful for his mom's guidance.

PLAYGROUND SAFETY

The importance of playground safety and how to stay safe while playing.

Playground Safety Heroes

There were two best friends named Emma and Jake who loved to play at the playground. They loved to swing, slide, and climb on the equipment.

One day, they noticed a younger child who was not following the playground rules. The child was running on the equipment, pushing other children, and not waiting for their turn.

Emma and Jake knew that this was not safe and wanted to do something about it. They approached the child and calmly explained the rules of the playground. They told the child that they needed to wait their turn, not push other children, and be careful while playing.

The child listened and started to follow the rules. Emma and Jake felt proud of themselves for being playground safety heroes and making the playground a safer place.

From that day on, Emma and Jake made sure to always follow the playground rules and remind others to do the same. They knew that playground safety was important not just for their own safety but for the safety of all children.

They also learned about the importance of using playground equipment properly and being aware of their surroundings. They made sure to always look for potential hazards and report any broken or damaged equipment to the playground staff.

HOME SAFETY

The importance of home safety and how to stay safe while at home.

Home Safety Superheroes

There were siblings named Alex and Mia who loved spending time at home. They liked to play games, watch movies, and cook with their parents.

One day, while their parents were away, Alex and Mia decided to bake some cookies. They turned on the oven and waited for it to preheat.

However, they forgot to use oven mitts when they took the cookie sheet out of the oven. They burned their hands and started to cry.

Luckily, they knew what to do in case of an emergency. They ran their hands under freezing water and put a wet cloth on them to ease the pain. They also called their parents, who came home right away and took care of their burned hands.

From that day on, Alex and Mia knew that it was important to always practice home safety. They learned about the dangers of hot surfaces and how to use oven mitts while handling hot objects.

They also learned about other home safety measures such as never leaving the stove unattended while cooking, using smoke detectors, and locking doors and windows.

Alex and Mia became home safety superheroes and made sure to always follow the safety rules to keep themselves and their family safe while at home.

EMERGENCY PREPAREDNESS

The importance of having an emergency preparedness plan and knowing what to do in case of an emergency.

The Emergency Preparedness Plan

There was a family who lived in a house in a small town. One day, a storm hit the town and knocked down power lines, leaving many homes without electricity.

The family realized that they were not prepared for such an emergency. They did not have a plan and did not know what to do. They felt scared and helpless.

However, they knew that they needed to act. They gathered and planned. They decided to gather food, water, and blankets in case they lost power for a long time. They also charged their phones and made sure to have a first aid kit handy.

Thanks to their emergency preparedness plan, the family was able to stay safe and comfortable while they waited for the power to come back on.

From that day on, the family knew that it was important to always have an emergency preparedness plan and to know what to do in case of an emergency. They learned about several types of emergencies, such as storms, fires, and earthquakes, and how to respond to each situation.

They also made sure to always have supplies such as food, water, and a first aid kit on hand in case of an emergency. They felt empowered, knowing that they were prepared for any situation that might come their way.